cloverleaf books™
Space Adventures

To the Stars!

Gina Bellisario

illustrated by Mike Moran

SCHOLASTIC INC.

For Milla, who lights up
my world—G.B.

No part of this publication may be reproduced, stored in a retrieval system, or transmitted in any form or by any means, electronic, mechanical, photocopying, recording, or otherwise, without written permission of the publisher. For information regarding permission, write to Millbrook Press, a division of Lerner Publishing Group, Inc., 241 First Avenue North, Minneapolis, MN 55401.

ISBN 978-1-338-21381-2

Text and illustrations copyright © 2017 by Lerner Publishing Group, Inc. All rights reserved. Published by Scholastic Inc., 557 Broadway, New York, NY 10012, by arrangement with Millbrook Press, a division of Lerner Publishing Group, Inc. SCHOLASTIC and associated logos are trademarks and/or registered trademarks of Scholastic Inc.

The publisher does not have any control over and does not assume any responsibility for author or third-party websites or their content.

12 11 10 9 8 7 6 5 4 3 2 1   17 18 19 20 21 22

Printed in the U.S.A.   40

First Scholastic printing, September 2017

Main body text set in Slappy Inline
Typeface provided by T26

TABLE OF CONTENTS

Chapter One
Star Girl.....4

Chapter Two
Giants and Dwarfs.....8

Chapter Three
Draco the Dragon.....14

Chapter Four
A Shooting Star.....18

Make a Nebula....22

Glossary....23

To Learn More....24

Index....24

Chapter One
Star Girl

We're going to explore space! Dad helps me set up my telescope. "Are you ready, Stella?" Dad asks.

"Star Girl is ready!" Star Girl is my explorer name. Every night, Dad and I go on a mission to space. Dad is my sidekick, Captain Dad. He's also an astronomer.

"What should we explore tonight?" Dad wonders.

All stars belong to a galaxy. The name of our galaxy is the Milky Way.

"The stars!" I say. "I want to see what they look like up close!"

Dad opens his astronomy book to a picture of a star. "A star is a ball of plasma," he says. "Plasma is hot, so it gives off light. That's why a star shines."

Chapter Two
Giants and Dwarfs

My rocket stops at the closest star to Earth—the sun!

Captain Dad pops up on the rocket's computer. "Better cover your eyes, Star Girl! Remember, a star glows brightly."

"A star burns the gas it's made from," Captain Dad says. "That gas is the star's fuel."

That reminds me to check my rocket's fuel tank. It's full. Whew! "Can a star run out of fuel, like a rocket?" I ask.

"When a star cools down, it shrinks into a white dwarf," Captain Dad says. "But a huge star—one that's much bigger than the sun—can explode. It can even leave a black hole behind."

Gravity in a black hole is very powerful. It pulls everything inside it. Not even light can escape it!

Giants? Dwarfs? "Stars sound like they come from fairy tales," I say. "Maybe I'll see a dragon!" Captain Dad smiles. "Look over there . . ."

Chapter Three
Draco the Dragon

I'm face-to-face with a dragon. It's made of stars!

Constellations are named after ancient stories. In one story, Draco was the pet of a goddess named Hera.

"That's Draco the dragon," Captain Dad says. "Draco is a constellation. That's a group of stars that form a pattern."

I think I'll take a break from exploring to play my favorite game: connect the stars!

"Wow, that star is really bright!" I point to the brightest star in the constellation Ursa Minor. "That's the North Star," Captain Dad says. "It shows which direction is north. Sailors once used constellations to find their way across the ocean."

Suddenly, a strange light shoots out of Draco's mouth. It's getting brighter and heading my way!

Chapter Four
A Shooting Star

ZOOM! The rocket flies back toward Earth. The light follows and blurs past us. "I know what that is. It's a shooting star!"

"A shooting star is actually a meteor," Captain Dad says. "It's the light from a burning space rock flying past Earth, but it's not the only thing that races around the universe."

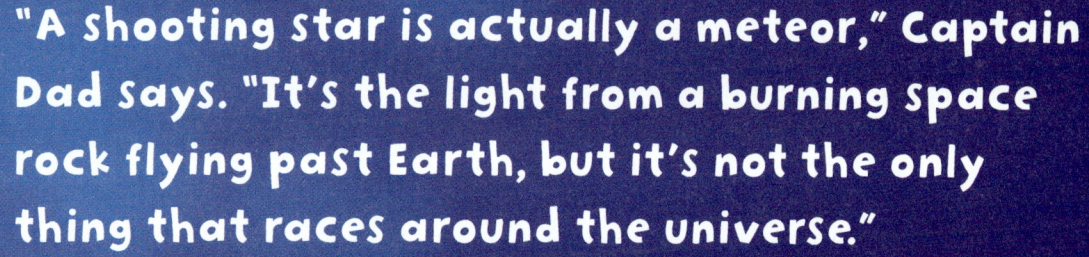

When a meteor crashes into Earth, it is called a meteorite.

19

A comet with a long tail sails through the sky. "A comet orbits the sun," Captain Dad says. "Comets are made of frozen gas and dust, so they're also called dirty snowballs."

"How about a space race: Star Girl versus the comet!" I say. But then I feel a kiss on my head, and I'm back in my room.

"I'm afraid our mission is done for tonight, Stella," Dad says. "It's bedtime."

I can't believe how much there is to know about stars. In fact, I'm going to race a shooting star in my dreams. First, I better fuel up my rocket!

Make a Nebula

Where is a star born? In a nebula! It's a cloud of gas and dust in space. A nebula can create hundreds of stars. In the starlight, a nebula can look as if it is different colors. You can make your own nebula!

What You Will Need
food coloring
a plastic water bottle
(half-full of water)
a pencil
cotton balls
silver glitter

How to Make a Nebula

1) Squeeze food coloring into the water bottle. Mix the coloring and water together.

2) Next, add a "cloud." Use the pencil to push some cotton balls into the dyed water. Make sure you add enough cotton to soak up the water.

3) Now sprinkle in "stars." Pour in the glitter. Then shake the bottle to spread the glitter around.

4) Add more water, and repeat steps 1 to 3 until your bottle is full. When you're done, display your nebula. That way, you can look at the stars all day—not just at night!

GLOSSARY

astronomer: a scientist who studies objects in the universe

expand: to get bigger

galaxy: a group of stars and planets

gravity: a force that pulls things toward one another

meteor: the streak of light made by a burning space rock when it flies past Earth

plasma: a heated mixture of gases and energy

telescope: an instrument that is used to see objects in the universe

TO LEARN MORE

BOOKS
Hughes, Catherine D. *First Big Book of Space.* Washington, DC: National Geographic, 2012. Explore the stars, comets, and more objects in space in this book.

Rajczak Nelson, Kristen. *20 Fun Facts about Stars.* New York: Gareth Stevens, 2015. Find out how scientists study stars. You can even look at a star chart.

Shepherd, Jodie. *To the Sun!* Minneapolis: Millbrook Press, 2017. Learn more about the closest star to Earth.

WEBSITES
Hubble Space Telescope
https://www.spacetelescope.org/images/viewall
This website has pictures that were taken by a space telescope. Look at a galaxy, black hole, nebula, and more.

NASA Space Place
http://spaceplace.nasa.gov/starfinder/en
Make a star finder, play a game, and find out which constellations you can see this month.

PBS Kids
http://pbskids.org/video/?guid=20a34cb5-d65b-42e5-a740-6f38a0a446b5
Watch this video to learn why the sun is a super star.

INDEX

comet, 20

constellations, 14–17

gas, 10, 20, 22

meteor, 19

plasma, 6

shooting star, 18–19, 21

sun, 8, 12, 20